This book was donated by a school psychologist

School Psychologists help
school-aged children
(and their families)
with social, emotional,
behavioral, and academic
wellbeing.

We work in schools,
private clinics, hospitals,
community care centers,
college campuses, and more!

nasponline.org

In Honor

of my father

JOHN S. WEINER

a

Fisherman

who rescued and adopted my two brothers and me

THE STORYTELLER

THE FISHERMEN and the MERMAIDS

Copyright 2008
By Judith M. Ackerman

THE STORYTELLER BOOKS
Fort Lauderdale, Florida 33317
Printed in the USA

Library of Congress Catalog-in-Publication Data
The Fishermen and the Mermaids

Summary: a fictitious and adventurous tale involving the fishermen of the sea and
the mystery of the mythical mermaids, leads one to ask the
unsolved question, are mermaids real?

ISBN 978-0-9980439-0-6

THE
FISHERMEN
AND THE
MERMAIDS

Written by
Judith M. Ackerman

Illustrations by
Kristina Wheeat

DO YOU BELIEVE IN MERMAIDS?

I never believed in them before. I thought they were fictional characters created for the purpose of fairytales and movies. But I have changed my mind, and I will tell you why.

You see, my father was a fisherman. He was the captain of a very large fishing vessel called a dragger. His name was John, but all of the other fishermen called him *"Murf."* He was tall and handsome with black curly hair. His complexion was ruddy from the wind and the salt water beating against his face. His muscles were big and strong from pulling the nets and hauling the fish into the hull of the ship, and I loved him.

The life of a fisherman was not an easy one. They worked on large fishing boats with huge nets called trawls, which dragged along the bottom of the ocean, gathering whatever fish and marine life that came into its path. Large engines hoisted the heavy nets up from the waters, dropping its catch onto the deck. There the fishermen would select the choicest fish for market. Sometimes they caught turtles and stingray, and even great white sharks!

The sea can be very dangerous, but my father was never afraid. He respected its powerful nature and knew its heavenly creator.

As a young boy, he fell in love with its beautiful sunrises and sunsets, the magical moonlight and the millions of twinkling stars, the discovery of its magnificent marine life and the enchanting calls of the seagulls, beckoning him to enter their world.

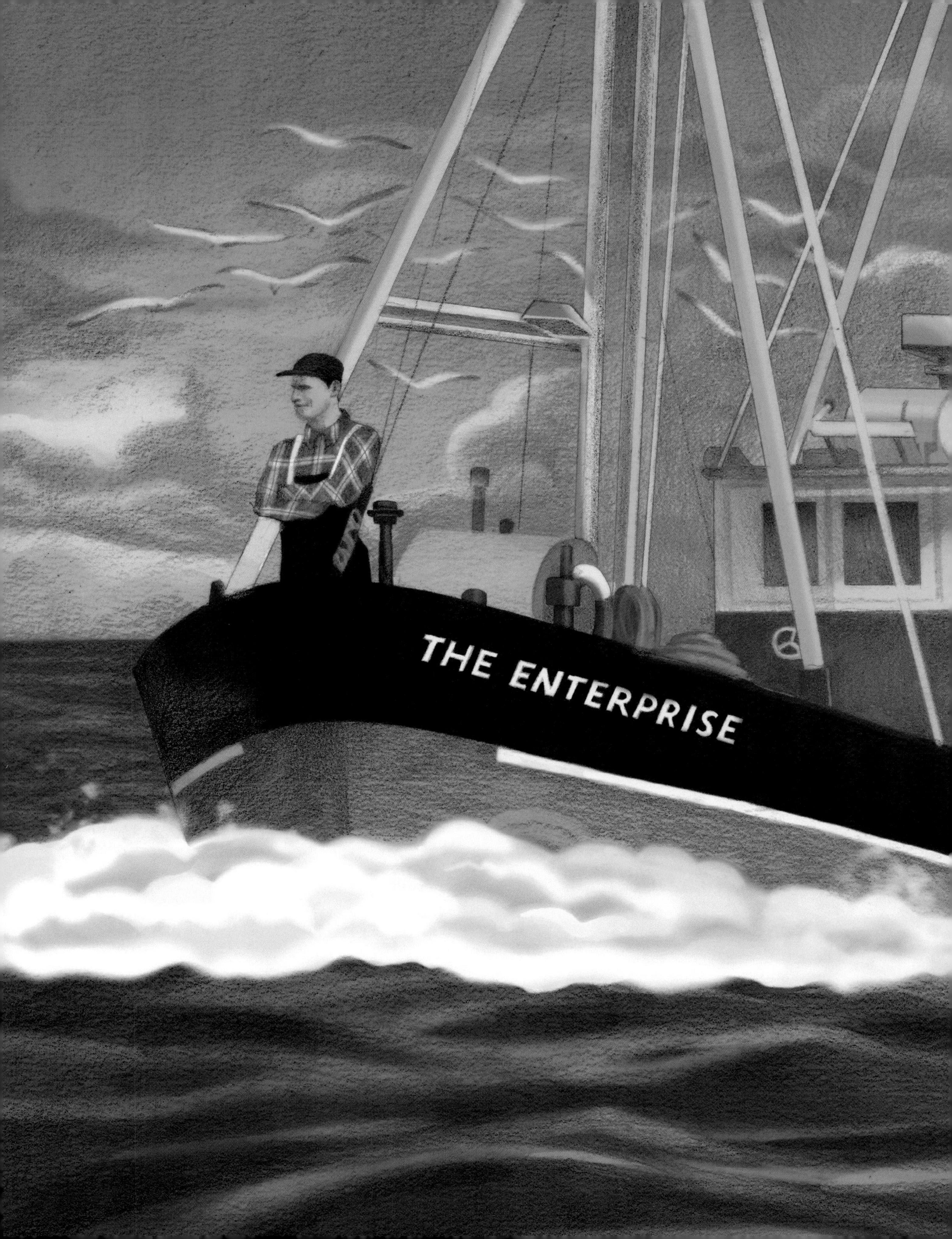
THE ENTERPRISE

There was no greater peace when the sea was calm, and nothing was more terrifying than when there was a storm. One moment it was calm and peaceful, the next moment, the sea could be angry and destructive. And my father loved it all.

Every time my father returned from the sea, my mother, brothers, sisters and I would wait eagerly to hear of his adventures. He would tell us about the beautiful creatures they caught in their nets and the terrifying experiences they had when a storm arose. Squalls would reach as high as sixty feet as they came crashing upon the deck. Thunder and lightning taunted them with fear as the torrid rains threatened to sink their ship. But in the morning, calm and peace would return once again. Peace, as if there had never been a storm, and the fishermen would fall in love with the sea all over again.

Once a man became a fisherman, nothing could keep him away from the beautiful but temperamental sea. It beckons them, just like the mermaids.

"Oh yes." I said, *"Mermaids!"*

My father would tell us stories of how the mermaids called out to the fishermen in the middle of the night. One might say it is probably just the wind, but every fisherman I know, swears that the mermaids call them by their names. Softly, gently, as the ship rocks them to sleep, as a mother rocks her baby, the mermaids would whisper their names and appear to them in their dreams.

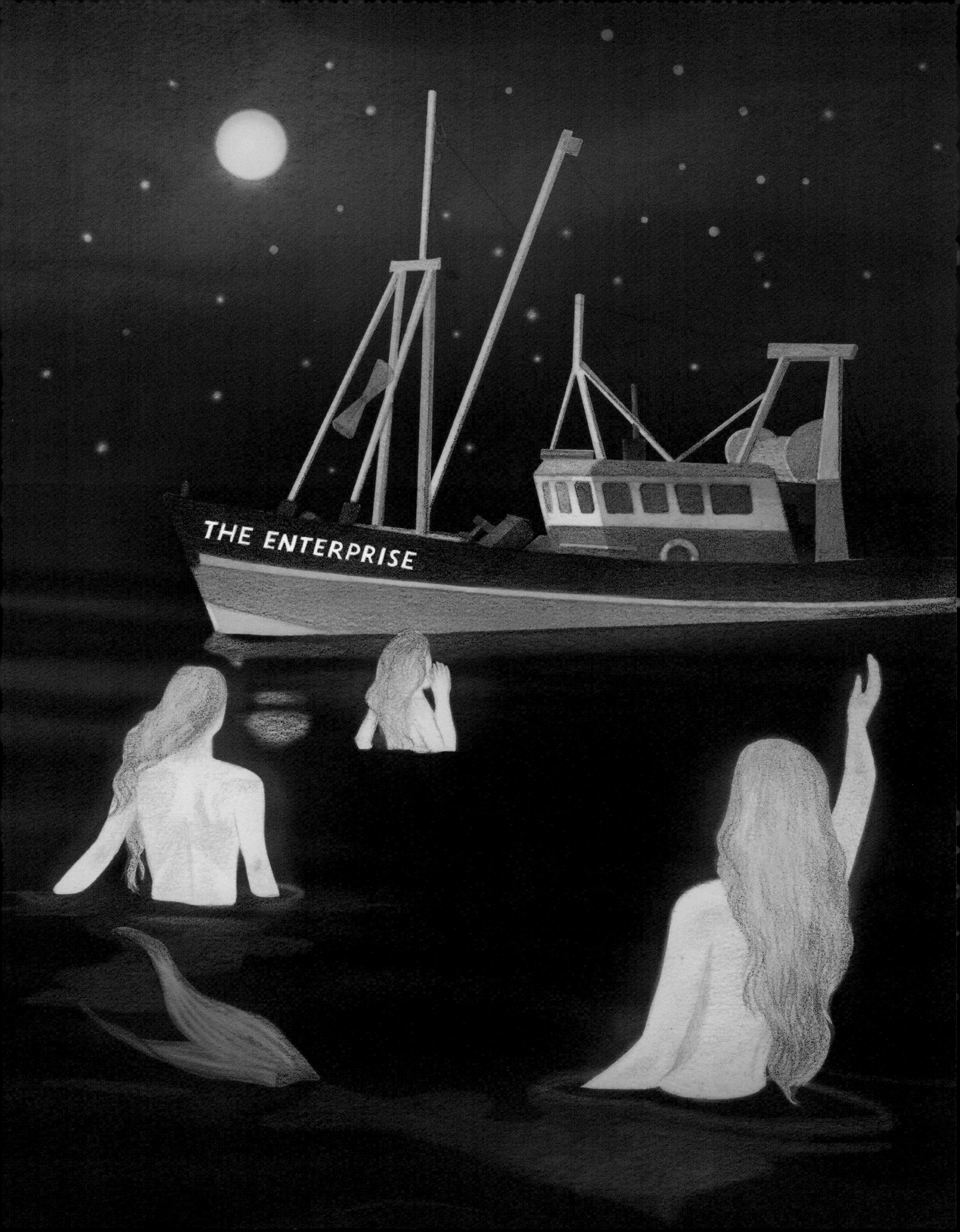
THE ENTERPRISE

Sometimes in the early morning, when the sun is glistening and dancing upon the water, the mermaids can be spotted playfully swimming with the dolphins. No one has ever caught a mermaid or even taken their picture, but each and every fisherman will swear that the mermaids are real.

I honestly had my doubts! I really thought that it was just another fish tale, until one night, my mother received a phone call that changed my mind forever.

The coastguard from New York City called to tell my mother that my father was alright. You see, his ship had gone aground in the middle of the night. It ran into some rocks, causing the bow to break in two.

The ship was sinking fast, and the three scared fishermen were forced to swim for their lives. My father managed to call the coastguard before they abandoned the ship, but they were three miles from the shore, and it did not look as if they could survive. As the waves pounded upon them, pulling them under over and over again, they knew they would not make it safely to the shore.

They prayed that the coastguard would soon arrive, but they didn't and were nowhere in sight. Not a glimmer of light could be seen in the pitch black night. There seemed to be no hope. The sea was too rough, and their muscles were too weak.

Just as they were ready to give up and surrender to the sea, three beautiful mermaids came beside them and gently held them in their arms. Swiftly, they swam, pushing through the crushing waves, delivering the fishermen safely to the edge of the shore.

Just as quickly as they appeared to save them, they quickly disappeared. Weak and exhausted, the fishermen laid on the beach, too weak to show their gratitude or even wave to the mermaids as they swam away.

The coastguard arrived moments later, surprised to find the fishermen alive, and wondered how they could have swum that far?

Would the fishermen explain how they were rescued? Would they tell the coastguard how the mermaids held them in their arms and delivered them safely to the shore? Surely, they would never believe them! Would they risk being laughed at, or would they claim they heroically and miraculously swam three miles from their sinking ship?

They told the truth, of course, and as the coastguard laughed in disbelief, the fishermen wondered, *"Do the mermaids only appear to the fishermen of the sea?"*

Not another word was spoken as the fishermen returned to the safety of their homes.

You would think this would be the end of the story and
the fishermen would never want to return to the sea.
But from the stories my father told me, I understood
and knew, the beautiful and unpredictable sea would
haunt each and every one of them; beckoning them
to return once again, in hopes of seeing the
mermaids who rescued them from their
beautiful, enchanting sea.

"NOW DO YOU BELIEVE IN MERMAIDS?"